A Tomcat's Tale

Library of Congress Cataloging-in-Publication Data

Johansen, Hanna, date
    [Felis, Felis. English]
    A tomcat's tale / Hanna Johansen; with illustrations by Käthi Bhend;
translated from the German by Susanna Fox.
        p.   cm.
    Translation of: Felis, Felis.
    Summary: Felis, a pet cat, tries in vain to educate the ignorant
humans who house and feed him, while seeking adventure by night
with the other cats in the neighborhood.
    ISBN 0-525-44583-8
    1. Cats—Juvenile fiction. [1. Cats—Fiction.] I. Bhend, Käthi, ill.
II. Title.
PZ10.3.J56To   1991   [Fic]—dc20   90-39067   CIP   AC

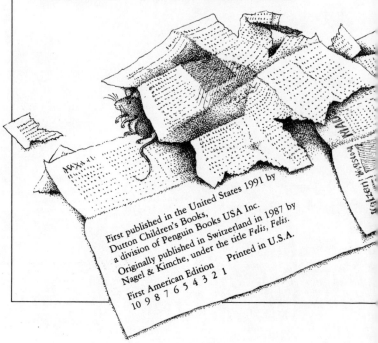

First published in the United States 1991 by
Dutton Children's Books,
a division of Penguin Books USA Inc.
Originally published in Switzerland in 1987 by
Nagel & Kimche, under the title *Felis, Felis.*

First American Edition   Printed in U.S.A.
10 9 8 7 6 5 4 3 2 1

A TOMCAT'S TALE
by Hanna Johansen

translated from the German by Susanna Fox

with illustrations by
Käthi Bhend

DUTTON CHILDREN'S BOOKS
NEW YORK

Chapter 1

"Felis, Felis!"

It was a rustling spring morning, already quite warm and still, at least as far as the birds' singing was concerned. A Sunday, in other words.

"Felis, Felis!"

"Finally," sighed Felis, who had been lying on top of the garden wall, rapt in thought, occasionally turn-

ing an ear to the blackbirds overhead or to a car driving away in the distance. "It must be past ten." The sun was already shining over the top of the neighbor's roof.

On Sundays, Felis always had to wait longer than usual. But this Sunday it had been at least ten minutes too long. He sprang to his feet without stopping to stretch, and was running swiftly toward the house when the woman called for a third time.

"Felis, Felis!"

What she neglected to say, of course, was this: Felis, we have finally woken up and stretched, we have come downstairs, and your breakfast is ready.

"Good morning," Felis said. "I'm glad you're up." He pressed his head and hip against her leg, fell down onto his side, and added, "It's truly a pleasure to see you." (Whenever he greeted her like this, she sat down beside him and scratched him wherever he liked best to be scratched.)

After a couple of minutes, Felis rose to his feet and remarked, "I'm sure you have already noticed that it's an exceptionally beautiful day."

The woman stood up, too, but said nothing.

Felis had a nagging suspicion that sometimes his people didn't seem to understand him when he spoke to them. Sometimes they acted like all he ever said was *meow*. He was sure that this misunderstand-

ing wasn't a result of ill will or even indifference—
he figured it was simply because their ears were too
small. Everything else on humans had turned out
quite large—everything but their ears.

"Come and eat," said the woman, and they entered
the house.

The man was waiting in the hallway. Felis stopped
in front of him and stretched first his forelegs, then
his hind legs—not too slowly, not too quickly, but
in just the right way.

"Greetings," Felis added, although he didn't really
have to.

"Greetings to you, too," said the man.

And, finally, it was time to eat.

Chapter 2

As it grew dark, Felis dozed on his green pillow, lost in fur-raising dreams which occasionally woke him up. Confused, he would look around the room until he recognized everything, then he would shut his eyes once again and listen to the ticking of the clock, the humming of the refrigerator, and the rattling of the water pipes until he fell back to sleep.

The more deeply a tomcat sleeps, the more he hears. Of course, he doesn't really hear more, he hears less—that is to say, he doesn't hear the clock,

the refrigerator, or the pipes; he hears the *important* sounds. Like tiny footsteps.

But since there never seemed to be any mice in Felis' house tiptoeing across distant rooms, he slept soundly and dreamlessly until a soft voice made his ears twitch. It seemed to have come from the barn in the back field, and it sounded like a tomcat.

Next Felis heard the voice coming from the garden. Now it was more than one voice, though; it was two tomcats, or three. And it was the same voices he had been hearing every night for a week. "You are big enough now," the tomcats called. "If you're going to live here with us, you're going to have to come out and show us who you are."

"Not today, thanks," Felis said, scratching himself behind one ear. What he wanted to do was to spend a quiet night on his green pillow, a long and undisturbed night. He didn't want to show anybody anything.

"Count me out," he said, scratching behind the other ear.

"What's taking you so long?" they called. "We can't wait out here all night."

Felis sighed. "Well, I suppose I'll have to go, then." He went to the door and said very clearly, "Open the door!"

"Oh, no, not again," grumbled the man, who was reading a book on the couch.

Felis sat down in front of the door.

"I know that you want your peace and quiet," Felis said. "But first you're just going to have to let me out."

Outside, the tomcats were still yowling.

The man said nothing.

Felis said nothing.

"I'll give him three minutes," thought Felis. "Five at the very most. Then he's going to sigh and get up."

The man sighed but he did not get up. Instead, he said, "Why don't you open the door yourself?"

"Hmm," said Felis.

"Other cats do that."

"I know. Other cats jump up to the handle and open the door. You've told me that many times. But I am who I am. And I don't think we cats are meant to open doors. It looks ridiculous."

The man sighed.

"You should be happy you can do me a favor," said Felis, very quietly and kindly.

"Felis, Felis." The man sighed, then got up and opened the door.

Felis was a brave tomcat. With a pounding heart, he slunk out into the clear night. He could make out

14

two tomcats. The spotted tom was sitting on the fence in the back; the white one sat somewhat closer. Both cats looked away, daring Felis to approach them.

Of course, it was absolutely unacceptable for these tomcats to be threatening him in his very own yard. No self-respecting yard owner should ever put up with such a thing. But for Felis, the issue was more than the yard. He wanted to show them that they couldn't just bully him around, night after night.

Now that he was a big cat, the other tomcats no longer played with him. Any friendly meetings had become a thing of the past—they all simply fought with one another. Although the others weren't actually bigger, they were older and knew how to take care of newcomers. "But that still doesn't give these guys the right to push me around," thought Felis.

He stopped at the big tree by the meadow and sharpened his claws against the bark so that the scratching could be heard far and wide. Even though the other tomcats pretended not to be watching, Felis knew they were impressed.

"Come on over here," Felis said when the white one finally lifted his head. "If you think you're stronger than I am, then think again."

The white tom stretched his hindquarters high, his stiff tail bent sharply down. He looked very big.

15

Then he thrust his head forward and turned his ears out—ever so slightly, but Felis knew what he meant. Felis did not allow himself to be intimidated. Whatever the white tom could do, Felis could, too.

And so they stood. Now and again one of them would take a few steps toward the other and then stop in his tracks. Slightly crouched, each tom got ready to pounce. Only the tips of their tails moved, steadily flicking from side to side.

When the white tom was at last a mere yard away, Felis cocked his head. The white tom snarled and lunged.

Felis flipped onto his back and grabbed the flying cat with his paws. The other cat dug his claws into Felis' fur, screeching loudly. They wrestled on the ground until suddenly they flew apart—immediately repositioning so that they were face to face again.

After the fourth round, Felis had had enough. He sat down to catch his breath, flattened his ears, and looked away. For a while the white tom maintained his stance, but eventually he too turned away and began sniffing the ground.

Felis, waiting for the white tom to leave, was infuriated. "What a nuisance," he thought. Finally, with the stiff legs of a runner who has just won a race, the white tom walked away.

"What a bully," Felis said to himself. "Goes away so I can quietly put my tail between my legs and run into the house. Well, he doesn't know me very well. I don't put my tail between my legs, and I don't run away. I'm going to stay right here, come what may."

But Felis was too excited to sit still for very long. He went over to the tree and sprayed its trunk. Next he started for the fence posts that surrounded his garden.

The spotted tom, who had been watching the fight from the fence, rose to his feet and stared Felis straight in the eye.

Felis immediately accepted the challenge. "This time I won't give up," he thought. The spotted tom jumped down. As they faced off—hindquarters lowered, ready to pounce, peering at each other through the narrowed slits of their eyes—Felis stiffened his ears. He attacked, landing on the other cat's stomach. The spotted one screeched and scratched, hitting out with his forepaws and kicking with his hind feet. Felis drew back, but immediately resumed a threatening position. He thought he detected a look of caution in the other tom's face.

Again, he atacked. But this time he did not let go. He paid no attention to the pain or to the blood running down his face. He roared a fierce battle cry.

The spotted tom hissed and spat to no avail. Slowly, Felis rose and gave his opponent an ominous look. This was one fight he could not lose. And indeed, the spotted cat lay still and flattened his ears, pulling in his head and refusing to look at Felis.

Felis stiffened his ears a bit more. But the other cat was finished.

"Well, that's it then," Felis said, turning away and sniffing around. Slowly he walked over to his tree. He heard the spotted tom jump to his feet and run off into the meadow.

"Now he knows what I'm made of," Felis thought proudly, and jumped onto the wall. He cleaned his face as best he could. His fur was matted. In vain, he tried to wipe away the pain in his ear. Then he curled up on his paws and listened to the rustling of the night.

Chapter 3

At seven the next morning, Felis went to the door and waited for it to be opened. He was hungry and his ear still hurt very much.

"Felis!" said the woman. "Felis, how dreadful. What happened?"

"What do you think happened?" Felis replied. "I chased away the spotted cat. He won't try to push me around anymore."

The woman called her husband.

The man said only one word: "Veterinarian!"

"No!" Felis cringed with fear. "Anything but that!"

The woman took him in her arms. He sniffed at her nose, and bit her gently on the chin. But he did so only half-heartedly. All he could hear, ringing in his ears, was *veterinarian, veterinarian, veterinarian. . . .*

"Poor Felis," said the woman.

"Put me down," said Felis. As long as the door was still open, he could make a run for it and hide. He gladly would have skipped breakfast, as long as he didn't have to go to the vet.

But it was too late. The man was already coming with the carrier. Together they stuck him inside and closed the lid. There!

Felis howled, "No! No!"

"Don't be afraid, cat," they said. Whenever they were trying to be especially nice to him, they called him "cat." Quite a nice name, too. But if they were trying to be so kind, why didn't they let him go and wait for his ear to heal by itself?

He heard the woman pick up her keys. He felt himself being lifted up in the carrier and taken outside. A dreadful clamor started up around him.

"Oh, no! Not that! I don't want to go!" Felis cried. His voice was even louder than the car's motor. "I don't want to ride in a car. I don't want to go to the vet."

The woman tried to calm him. "Don't be afraid, cat. Your ear looks awful. It's torn to pieces. You can get very sick from something like that."

"If it were up to me," Felis thought, "there wouldn't need to be any doctors. Isn't a fellow unhappy enough when he's sick?"

Felis howled.

"The veterinarian will help you," she said.

"She's crazy," Felis thought. "Help me! I hate this. And I hate the vet. He has a way of grabbing me so that I can't defend myself. One of these days I'll outsmart him—I'm sure of it. I'll get him, and will he ever be sorry then. I'll just have to be quicker than he is. I'll have to scare him. And then take off. No. I'll have to scare him and bite him to smithereens just the way a rat would. That's right—like a fat, brown rat. I'll scare him so much that he won't be able to see or hear. Then he'll never dare to touch me again, that's for sure. If only this car weren't so noisy."

In the waiting room, Felis sat quietly and looked around with wide, fearful eyes.

"Don't be afraid," the woman said again as he cowered on the examining table. And once again the vet was too fast for him.

"What a bunch of nonsense," thought Felis once he was back in his carrier. "What good does it do to dab around on an ear that already hurts, anyway? Plus it took forever. But I didn't give in. Didn't scream. Didn't howl."

They got back into the car. Felis knew they were going home, but the car made him furious, anyway. So furious that he didn't even think about his ear anymore. At home he went into the kitchen, sniffed his plate, and turned away. He didn't feel like eating after all that excitement. He didn't feel like talking, either. He lay down on his green pillow and curled up. Half asleep and half awake, he asked himself, "Why all that bother? My ear doesn't hurt the slightest bit anymore."

From this day on, Felis had a new name.

"Hey, Slit Ear!" they called him. This was his third name. Luckily he was smart enough to remember all three.

Chapter 4

The first day home from the vet's, Felis did not go outside. His people had left, and the usual daytime sounds filled the house. Felis felt thirsty. His bowl of water was in the kitchen, but he paid no attention to it.

At first he had tried drinking from it. He had glanced at the woman and said, "This water smells bad."

"Go ahead and drink it," she had replied. "It's fresh."

Every day it was the same. The water smelled bad and the woman wouldn't believe it.

Usually, when he could get outdoors, he drank from the birdbath. The water smelled better there. But since he had decided to stay at home that morning, he had to stay there all day. No one could open the door for him now that his people had gone to work. Felis scratched himself. "Maybe it wouldn't be

such a bad idea," he thought, "if I did learn how to open the door." He yawned. "Nonsense. Well, maybe they have forgotten to close a window." He sniffed. He looked around. Of course the windows were closed. How many times had he tried to tell them that at least one of the windows should be left open? But there was no talking to them on that point.

So Felis went back to the kitchen. *Drip. Drip. Drip.* Whenever the faucet leaked, Felis would jump into the sink and catch the drops with his tongue. It quenched his thirst, was much more fun, and the smell wasn't half as noticeable. (Of course he could only do that when he was alone.)

Outside, a dog was barking. Felis jumped from the sink where he had been drinking onto the table and looked out the window. (That was another one of those things he could do only when no one was home.) But nothing was happening outside. No dog to be seen and hardly any birds; only the leaves were moving. They fluttered and fluttered, yet they didn't seem to get anywhere. Felis grew sleepy watching the endless fluttering. Gradually the leaves grew more restless. "My fierce yellow eyes must be frightening them," thought Felis. The leaves pushed and pulled and tugged at their branches. Then, just to torment him, they jumped off the tree and floated

27

away. "Oh, well," said Felis. "I'll have to be faster next time."

Felis curled up to rest for a while on the newspaper that had been left on the table. Dozing off, he suddenly spotted something in front of him. "Well, well . . ." he thought. "If it isn't a mouse. . . ."

And it was a mouse. The mouse rose onto its hind legs and looked him straight in the eye.

"Don't look at me like that, " said Felis.

The mouse grinned. It had two sharp, white teeth.

Felis cringed. He didn't like it when mice showed their teeth.

"That's not how mice are supposed to act." The mouse was still grinning, but it looked as if it were getting ready to jump at his face and bite him.

"Ha!" squeaked the mouse.

"That's the last straw," said Felis. He crept a few steps closer and crouched down, preparing to pounce. The mouse went on leering. Felis pounced. But as he jumped, a crack in the table opened and the mouse dropped right through it!

"Well, if that isn't the nastiest trick around," Felis thought. "If I'd known he could do that, I'd have made my move much earlier." Now Felis had no other choice but to stick his paw into the crack and try to force the mouse out. "You'll stop grinning soon enough, Mouse," he said happily when his paw

touched something soft. But no matter how far Felis stretched, he couldn't catch the mouse. He sat up and waited. He could sit in front of a mouse hole for a very long time. He was in no hurry. But this time, although he waited a long, long time, there was just no mouse to be seen.

"I might as well rest my eyes a bit," thought Felis.

He was awakened by a sharp pain in his ear.

"That stupid mouse bit me," he mumbled, a bit surprised that he hadn't heard its footsteps approaching. But he did catch one glimpse of it as it jumped back through the crack. And so he sat back down in front of the crack to fish around some more.

"It's no use," he finally decided.

Then he thought of something. If a mouse suddenly disappeared through a crack in the table, where would that mouse be? Where else but under the table!

Felis jumped down, prowled around the legs of the table, and sniffed every square inch of the floor. No smell of mouse anywhere.

"Ha!" squeaked a voice over by the door. "You can't even hold the tip of your tail still."

"Now that does it." Felis shot forward. He clamped the mouse to the floor with one paw and braced his hind legs firmly, in case the mouse decided to put up a fight. Then he sank his teeth into

its neck. The mouse stopped moving. Felis sat up, looked around the room, and was surprised to find that he wasn't out in the field. Then he jumped onto the table with his catch.

He had hardly put the mouse down when he heard a pitter-pattering under the table. He looked down. Never in his life had he seen so many mice in one place. Felis jumped down and pounced on those closest to the door before they could get away. He piled them up, one by one, on the table. When he had caught ten, he began to get tired of his game. "These stupid mice," he thought. Soon he was letting the mice run closer and closer to him, even over his paws. Only when one tried to escape from the kitchen would he grab it and carry it back to the others as if it were a little kitten. He didn't feel like killing them anymore. He just wanted to sleep. Exhausted, he jumped on the table and stretched out on the newspaper. Dozens of mice followed him. Not much bothered by the constant pitter-patter of their feet, Felis got up and took a lazy swipe at the mice only when they dared to nibble his ears.

Next thing he knew there was a key in the door.

Felis opened his eyes. How could he not have heard the bus? And more importantly, where were all the mice? Piles of mice, everywhere, gone. Felis sighed. At least one or two could have been the real thing.

Felis always heard the two o'clock bus. Then it would take him just the right amount of time to rise, stretch, and assume his position by the front door to greet the woman. But this time he barely had a chance to jump down from the table before she entered the house. "She couldn't possibly have seen me on the table," he thought. Felis stretched out to greet her. "And it's too bad—she would have been so happy to see all of those mice."

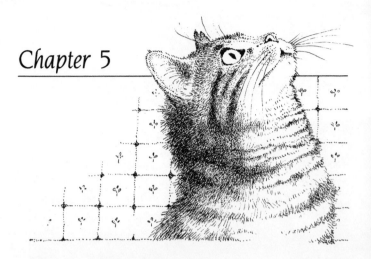

Chapter 5

The front door was not opened that evening. "No," they said. "Not tonight and not tomorrow, either. You need some peace and quiet."

"Well, I suppose they're right about that," thought Felis. They had carried him into the kitchen on his green pillow and closed the door. And so he had to spend the whole, long night in the kitchen—where things could get very, very boring. He hoped there'd at least be a fly. A cat who is locked in a room with a fly has plenty to do. Felis listened. No fly.

There wasn't even a rug with edges to burrow into and chew.

This was more peace and quiet than he needed.

"Okay," he thought, "you can lie around on the table and jump up onto the windowsill, the refrigerator, and the top of the closet. That's all very well. But you can't tell me that's interesting for more than half an hour."

His people were sleeping. Or maybe they weren't? He heard footsteps in the hallway.

"Would you please be so kind as to open the door for me?" said Felis.

No answer.

"Hey, open the door!" he repeated so loudly that not even a human ear could miss it.

But it didn't help at all. They didn't want him running around the house while they were sleeping. And unfortunately they always slept at night, just when he was never very tired. Above all, they didn't want him to sit in front of their door meowing because he wanted to come in and jump into their bed. Heaven only knows why not, but that's just the way they were. Felis had come to accept this.

"Open the door!" he called one last time when things had become quiet again.

Felis jumped onto the refrigerator and tried to see out of the window. He was bored. But a smart tomcat never stays bored for very long. He wraps his paws around his head and falls asleep.

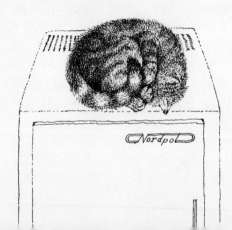

The following morning, when he wanted to go out into the yard, the answer was again no.

"But my ear doesn't hurt at all anymore," Felis protested.

Nevertheless, he had to stay at home.

In the spring, when it was warm, Felis would hunt during the noontime hours. He hunted in the yard, in the neighbor's field, or in the back on the hill, as long as the other, older cats weren't there.

But whenever he had to stay indoors, like today, he hunted there. He chased his white ball around and went crashing up the stairs as soon as the ball began to fight back. He pounced on newspapers. (And newspapers certainly don't put up with just anything. Whenever they tried to attack him from above, he mustered up all his strength and ripped them apart with great swipes of his paw.)

Once he had even jumped up on the windowsill and dug the soil out of the flowerpots. His people had been furious. He had heard a loud *no* as they dropped him rather ungently to the floor. "No more of that—it's not worth it," he had thought, and never even glanced at the windowsill again.

When Felis was young, he had also liked to sharpen his claws on the sofa. But his people hadn't liked that either. "And I have to agree with them," he thought. "That was childish." Scratching the bark of trees, on the other hand, was an entirely different matter. "Aaaah!" Felis thought wistfully, looking out of the window. "For a good tree to scratch!" But all he could do was watch and wait for the two o'clock bus.

Finally the woman came home. She greeted him, then immediately started to dash around the house. "She really should sit down and relax for a moment," Felis thought.

When she came to brush off the sofa he purred and said, "Meow!"

She stroked his head with her hand and continued her cleaning.

"Meeow!"

Nothing.

"Sometimes these humans are enough to drive you up a wall," thought Felis. "As usual, she doesn't get it." (What Felis was really trying to say was, would you please sit down now so I can sit on your lap and purr and gently knead your stomach?)

"Meeeooow!" He began to purr.

The woman also said, "Meow, meow," and dashed up the stairs. Felis walked over to his green pillow and muttered to himself, "That really is the limit, when they start meowing, too."

"You have the life, cat," she said as she rushed

back downstairs. "You don't have to clean house, go to work, save any money, or do the shopping."

"You never have to go to the vet," he retorted. But she refused to listen to him.

Then the great racket began.

"Stupid vacuum cleaner," Felis grumbled and went as far away as he possibly could. In the farthest corner of the house, he fell asleep under a bed.

"Felis, where are you?"

He didn't answer. Only when he grew hungry did he return to the kitchen. Since the front door remained closed even after his meal, he retreated to his green pillow. But wait . . . what was that? Hadn't the edge of that rug just moved?

"Uh-oh," he said.

Startled, the edge of the rug fell still. But it had a funny way of looking at him. Felis gave it a nudge and it stood up on end.

"You'll soon regret that!" Felis said, and with one leap he jumped sideways at it and attacked it with all four paws. The rug was a tough opponent, however, and wouldn't easily admit defeat.

"With a rug, you really have to sink your teeth in," Felis thought as he wrestled. "It's not at all like fooling around with a friend." No, this rug was dangerous and had to die.

Felis at last sat up and looked at his victim.

"It looks dead, but it isn't. Or is it?"

The rug lay still.

"Maybe it's just pretending to be dead." Felis was too smart for that trick. He poked at it with his paw. There! No question about it—the edge of that rug was still alive, and Felis would have to attack again with all his might.

"Felis, Felis," said the woman, who was standing in the doorway watching him (even though she knew he hated to be watched).

Felis hid behind the chest of drawers and looked at her, ready to dash away if she moved just one step closer.

"The rug has gotten very fresh," he explained.

"Hey, Slit Ear," the woman said, "I think you have all sorts of nonsense in mind today."

"Of course I do," said Felis. "If I didn't have it in mind, where else would I have it? There'd be no sense to it at all. Nothing against nonsense, but if there's no sense in it, it's nonsense."

Chapter 6

When summer had passed and the days grew shorter and the winds cooler, things began to change. The nightly fights came to an end. The other tomcats became more peaceful, and so did Felis. They all knew where they stood with one another. Sometimes, toward midday, the white tom would come through the fence to look around the yard. Felis wouldn't stop him. It was clear who would win in the event of an argument. Felis lay on the wall and avoided looking in the white tom's direction, although nothing he did escaped Felis' attention. And when the visitor amicably lifted his tail as he passed by, Felis purred quietly.

Felis was less gracious with the other tomcats. He would ask them to leave, although he never made a big issue of it.

On this day, Felis lay on the wall in the sun and closed his eyes, feeling his fur grow pleasantly warm.

When the sun disappeared behind a few clouds, he got up and decided to make his usual rounds. Felis noticed new scratches on the post from the gray tom. The gray lived next door and liked to sharpen his claws on other cats' posts. There were no traces of any new scents.

Felis recognized all the scents in the neighborhood and knew who had left them; faint scents against which he rubbed his head to remind the others that he was the one who lived there, and stronger scents which he had to spray over.

After making his rounds, Felis crawled under the fence. He trotted a few steps to the right and then took the path across the meadow. But he didn't get far before he saw a she-cat approaching. It was the striped one. She was heading straight for the intersection of their two paths, and fortunately had not yet seen him. Felis sat down, examining the grass at his feet, and waited for the other cat to pass. Why should he cross her path? Then they'd have to greet each other. And after that, who knew what she'd do!

And so he waited until the striped cat passed ahead of him and disappeared. Then he walked on. He had to cross the quiet street where the white tomcat lived. Felis went into the yard to pay him a visit, but no one was home. So he sprayed a strong Felis-scent against the fence as a sign that he had been there. Then he continued on until he came to the big, sloping meadow by the hill.

This was free territory; everyone used it. The meadow was dotted with a few tree stumps and circled by a hedge where you never had to wait long for a mouse to appear. And if no mouse appeared, at least you could count on a beetle. Filled with anticipation, Felis approached the hedge. That's when he noticed the gray tomcat—the one cat in the whole neighborhood that Felis didn't like.

"Just my luck," he thought. "I should have come earlier."

But he didn't feel like turning back right away, so he sat down for a moment. The gray one seemed to have discovered something. He looked ready to pounce. But then he noticed that Felis was watching,

and the gray tom paused. Instead of striking the grass with his lifted paw, he licked it. And since Felis continued to watch him, the gray kept washing himself: his legs, his shoulders, his sides—so thoroughly that it seemed he'd never had anything else in mind in the first place. But he didn't go away.

If it had been early in the morning, the gray tom would have made room for Felis. But since the afternoon light was already fading, the gray had the right to stay where he was—and Felis knew it. Felis greeted the other cat briefly, then changed his plans.

He decided to try the tin shed. On its roof was a spot that all the cats preferred, not only because it was warm, but because it offered an unusually good view of the neighborhood. Felis discovered, however, that because of the gray clouds, the spot on the roof was no longer warm. While he pondered what to do next, the wind began to whip at the fallen branches on the ground. Felis crouched down to watch them.

"Felis, Felis," he said to himself. "You're not going to start hunting these branches. Not here, where someone might easily see you." He pictured the scornful look on the spotted tom's face if he caught sight of Felis chasing around after dead branches. "No," Felis thought, "it's better just to go home."

The first drops of rain were already falling. Felis

45

waited under a woodpile for the shower to end. Then he went on his way.

But as soon as he arrived in his own yard, the sun burst through the clouds.

"If I had known that was going to happen," Felis thought, "I would have gotten up on the tin roof after all. Especially since I was the only one there." He sat down under the hazel bush and tried to decide whether or not to leave again. While he was thinking things over, he squinted up at the sky.

The sun sparkled through the branches, the raindrops sparkled on the leaves, the leaves trembled on the branches, the raindrops fell in the sun, and the branches trembled in the wind. And the raindrops sparkled on the leaves on the branches in the wind, until Felis' eyes dropped shut.

He found himself once again in a land where the sun sparkled through the branches and the raindrops sparkled on the leaves and the leaves . . .

"That's enough now," whispered Felis, falling into a deeper sleep, a sleep so deep that it was beyond the reach of dreams.

Usually Felis slept only when it was necessary. But sometimes he slept when he had nothing better to do. He slept deeply or lightly; sometimes he dreamed, sometimes he didn't. Felis loved all types of sleep.

"Felis! Felis!"

Dinner was ready, and it was something special tonight, something that smelled like fish. Tuna, in fact. After Felis had cleaned his plate and licked his chops, he lay down on the green pillow. But when he heard his people getting ready for bed, he asked them to open the door for him.

Felis headed straight for the big hill. It was late.

Sure enough, Felis was one of the last to arrive. The tomcat club had already assembled. Everyone was sitting peacefully in a circle, close together, but not so close as to bother one another. Felis walked toward his spot a little more quickly than usual, and the detour that he made around the gray tom was a little shorter than it should have been. In any case, the gray tom flattened his ears.

"You don't have to be so touchy," Felis hissed, planting himself in front of the gray tomcat.

"Just who do you think you are!" one of the other cats called out.

Felis turned around.

"Show-off!" called another.

"Oh, all right, all right," said Felis. As he walked on, he slowly lifted his tail and greeted the others politely, sniffing several noses that were turned toward him, until finally reaching his usual place.

And so they sat together on the hill. Sometimes

47

one cat would lick and wash another cat, just a little bit, as a sign of friendship and a way to pass the time pleasantly. Of course there was some hissing now and then, but only when someone forgot to keep his proper distance. Such incidents never led to any serious fighting—almost immediately, there were friendly faces and the chattering would continue.

These meetings could last for hours. If it started to rain, the cats quickly said good-bye. Otherwise, they usually went home around midnight. Felis' people would already be in bed, so he would lie down to sleep on the dry grass under the juniper bush.

Chapter 7

"Felis is sitting with his back to the radiator," said the man. "There's going to be a frost."

And there was a frost.

Winter came. Felis hesitated in the doorway before venturing out, testing the temperature. Not that he was cold. His coat of fur was always thick, but now it had grown even thicker.

This was his second winter. During his first winter he had been sick. His throat had been so sore that he couldn't eat anything (except grass, which was hard to find). After he had finally managed to eat a very large portion of grass, his throat had felt much better. This year Felis was healthy. Still, he often stayed home during the night, especially when it was stormy outside. He didn't like to feel the wind whipping through his fur.

Soon it began to snow. Thick snowflakes floated down from the sky, just waiting for someone to play with them. With stiff legs, Felis hopped about, trying to catch the fattest ones before they hit the ground.

One day, when the bitter cold of January had subsided and the days were sunnier and milder, Felis set out. He headed toward the hill. Even before he reached it, however, he realized that it wasn't the time to hunt or play. Something that he couldn't explain was propelling him forward.

Soon Felis had left his own neighborhood entirely. Everything looked unfamiliar; the houses, the yards. And wherever he sniffed, it smelled of strange cats. He didn't find his own scent anywhere.

Every now and then he would sit down to lick his feet, then get right back up again. He felt hungry, but he couldn't stop to eat. He didn't need any sleep, either. He felt prepared to go a long, long way.

Day came and then it was night again.

On one of the trees Felis found impressive scratch marks, obviously left by a very large tomcat. Normally this would have made him hesitate to approach unknown territory. But not this time. He was being drawn urgently forward, farther and farther, and nothing could stop him. Not even a passing dog distracted him.

And it was because of this that Felis never saw the car. He was running across a big street, looking straight ahead, when there was a sudden screech. The car swerved, skidded, and would have hit him—had he not in the last split second leaped to safety.

Badly shaken, Felis cowered beneath some bushes. But even before his heart had stopped pounding he was on his way again, forgetting his hunger, forgetting the cars, and forgetting anything that would have diverted him from his mission.

Sometimes on the stone posts separating the streets and the yards, Felis detected a certain scent. It was unlike any other he had ever smelled before. It smelled like a she-cat—not like any of the ones

that he knew back home, but a special she-cat. Even the lampposts, the tree trunks, and the hubcaps on cars smelled of her. He sniffed and ran and sniffed and ran.

Felis knew that she was trying to signal him. Her scent was getting very strong now. And finally, Felis traced it to one particular yard.

He quickly realized that he was not the only tom who had been called by the scent. As he crept into the she-cat's yard, he immediately spied another tomcat, busying himself near the back. A skinny, mean-looking tomcat.

"Just what do you think you're doing here?" Felis hissed.

The tomcat rose to his feet and walked a few steps in Felis' direction. "Why don't you get lost," he replied.

But Felis had not come this far for nothing. The she-cat had called him alone, and Felis knew it. If the other tomcat didn't leave immediately, Felis would have to show him the way.

The intruder, a wiry little creature with a determined look, appeared not to think twice about leaving. He stretched his hind legs. Every single hair on his back stood up on end. Turning slightly to the side, he suddenly loomed very large and threatening.

But Felis wasn't one to be easily intimidated. He

53

puffed out his own tail and confidently stretched it into the air.

It was at that moment that Felis saw the she-cat. She had a shiny black coat, green eyes, and moved very gracefully. She looked back at Felis briefly and rubbed her head against a door. Then she walked a few steps and dropped onto her side.

The two tomcats turned their attention back to each other.

Stiff-legged, they circled each other, snarling and growling with excitement. Next they faced off, their ears sharply pricked and the tips of their tails twitching. A battle cry rose from Felis and faded again.

Suddenly each went for his opponent's neck, but both were too quick to be wounded on the first strike. They jumped at each other, rolling over and over while biting and scratching and kicking.

The fighting went on endlessly, or so it seemed to Felis. Already exhausted from his journey, he finally couldn't take any more.

"Ten points for you," Felis said, and sat up to lick his paws. Humiliated, he watched the winner strut away.

After a few minutes' rest, Felis stood up to leave. But just as he was slipping through the bushes, the she-cat quietly called to him.

"Come with me," she said and ran off in the other direction.

Felis watched her for just a moment, unsure—then he made up his mind, and followed. Cutting through the backyard, they slipped through a hole in the fence and disappeared together into the field.

At noon, Felis found himself alone again, sitting in the she-cat's backyard. He heard her voice once. She was in the house, and the front door was closed. Then he heard nothing more.

Felis felt his stomach growl. "I have to get something to eat," he thought. His own house was very far away—he would have to forage for food. Luckily, before he had gone very far he detected a most promising scent. It smelled of a kitchen, of meat and fish. And directly beside this kitchen was a little shed with three big trash cans in it. Two were shut with lids, but the third was open. Felis jumped up and saw that it was filled to the top with leftover vegetables, lettuce leaves, and scraps of meat. He fished out a pork chop and carried it to a protected place in the yard. Then he ate every last shred of meat, washed himself, and fell into a deep, deep sleep.

Chapter 8

Felis slept deeply, but not for long. He wanted to get back to the she-cat. Finding her yard again was easy; he followed her scent down the big road until he recognized the house.

Along the way, he came upon a tomcat lying in the middle of the road.

"Get lost," Felis snarled.

The tomcat didn't move, not even when Felis approached him menacingly. Felis sniffed the air and stepped closer. Something was not quite right. The tomcat's fur was matted with blood, and his eyes stared straight ahead, glassy and unseeing.

A car thundered past in the other lane. Felis sprang to the side of the road, shook himself, and quickly went on.

He looked around the she-cat's yard. Nobody was home. Softly he began calling to her, then so loudly that even if she were in the house, she would have to hear him. But there was still no answer. He sat down to wait.

Finally, in the gray of dawn he heard a soft cry. The she-cat returned on quiet paws, walking right up to him and licking his nose in greeting. Then she lay down at his side, and they slept.

Days passed and Felis stayed with the she-cat. When her people didn't disturb them, they spent all their time together. When she had to go in the house, Felis called to her. And if she didn't come out, he ventured on to a yard he had found where he could eat and sleep.

But gradually, things changed between them. She still greeted Felis when he came over. She still purred. She didn't even mind if he washed himself and lay under her bushes. But she stopped luring him—her scent had lost all its charm for him. To Felis, she smelled like cat and that was all.

The new yard he had found was a good place to be. He had much more land than at home. In fact, it wasn't really a yard, but a park—a whole park that belonged to him. Felis had plenty of time to explore his park—its bushes, steps, flower beds, and lawns.

There were also many humans who walked along the park paths and paused to chat with him. Felis liked humans. He liked his people at home the best, of course, but he liked strangers, too. Some took almost no notice of him, but others seemed so happy to see him he figured they had come just for that purpose.

Every day, a little after noon, leftovers were brought from a big house on the edge of the park and dumped into trash cans. Felis rummaged around until he found something he liked. After eating, he found a place to nap.

Usually the sun shone warmly through the bare branches of the trees, but one day there was no sun at all and it grew very, very cold. The park was deserted. A strong wind whipped the lawn where Felis normally lazed for hours, waiting for mice. Felis felt chilly and needed to get warm. He remembered his home, his people, his cozy green pillow by the radiator and he wished he were dozing there, waiting for

the sound of the can opener. Felis' stomach growled.
He had found nothing to eat that day—the three
trash cans at the big house had been tightly closed.
Felis crawled into a pile of leaves and shivered.

"Felis! Felis!"
Felis jumped to his feet. The voice was familiar.
He ran into the house and recognized his people.
They were standing in the kitchen with a huge plate
of sardines in front of them on the floor.

He was just about to dig in when he awoke with
a start. No house, no kitchen, no plate, no people.
Just a chilly field, smelling of wet, rotten wood. Felis
sighed. He wished he could have at least finished the
sardines.

"I really should go home soon," he thought. "That
would be the best thing." But Felis didn't remember
how to get to his real home, where his people lived.
It was in the same direction as the morning sun, and
that's all he knew.

Felis heard familiar church bells pealing in the distance. He listened closely. "That's just about where
it must be," he thought. "My house. Maybe I can
find it. But it's a long way off, and today it's too cold
for traveling." He yawned and fell asleep. But when
he woke up, he was even hungrier than before.

"Felis, Felis," he thought. "You've got to do something about this."

He ran to the big lawn behind the trees. Choosing one of the hundreds of mouse holes there, he sat down and didn't take his eyes off it. After half an hour he walked around the hole and sat down to watch it from the other side. There was no mouse to be seen.

After an hour, it got so bitter cold that Felis gave up. "I don't really like mice, anyway," he thought as he walked away. He searched all the houses on the street until he came to a window that had accidentally been left open. Felis listened closely, and when all seemed quiet he jumped up onto the window ledge. Cautiously, he peered into the kitchen. The smells of good things to eat filled his nostrils. A big plate of meat, even bigger than what Felis would have gotten at home, was sitting on the floor. Felis hopped down and began to eat greedily.

"Hey!" a voice suddenly shouted, loud and close by. "Hey!"

Felis saw the dark figure of a man overhead, and hands reaching out to grab him. With lightning speed, he turned and cleared the window in two leaps.

"If I ever catch you, you're going to get it!" the voice shouted after him. "You nasty thief!"

Felis ducked under some bushes, but behind them stood a wall. He had no choice but to double back and continue on in plain view. Before he made it out of the yard, a dog planted itself before him, a huge dog with threatening ears and bared teeth. A growling dog.

There was no turning back, nowhere to hide. Just one tree, and it was very far away. Felis acted quickly. Before the dog could attack, Felis jumped forward

and sunk his claws into the dog's face. The dog howled in pain. But Felis had already let go and was off and running with huge leaps. He had to reach the tree before the dog caught up with him. Three leaps more. Two. He was there! At the very last second, Felis grasped the trunk with his claws and scrambled up, higher and higher, until he came to a branch far above the ground.

Down below, the dog jumped and barked, wild

with rage. Felis surveyed the scene from his branch, his pounding heartbeat slowly returning to normal. Now all he had to do was wait.

The dog waited, too.

Dusk came and it grew dark. Both of them waited.

Finally a voice called out from the house. The dog perked up his ears and slowly strode away.

"Finally!" thought Felis.

Just to be on the safe side, however, he waited a little bit longer.

Exhausted and cold, Felis arrived back at the park. He crawled into his hiding place in the leaves and fell asleep.

The next day was warmer, but it stormed. Unceasingly, the rain poured through the trees. It didn't even stop long enough for Felis to dash out and find something to eat without getting completely soaked. Felis dozed and waited. He didn't mind. He had a talent for waiting.

But the rain lasted too long, even for someone who likes waiting. Days. Nights.

"Enough is enough," Felis finally said. "If this nasty rain doesn't stop soon, I'm going home."

But who would set out on a long trip in such bad weather? Not Felis. Never. A long trip is tiring enough, and a coat of soaked fur would make it unbearable.

"I'll wait," he decided. "When the rain stops, I'll go."

That evening it finally stopped. The air became dry. Felis stretched and left his hiding place to look around. "It sure is nice here," he said. "Why should I go home if it's not raining?"

Chapter 9

Spring had come.

A blackbird hopped across the grass. Felis crouched. The blackbird, who hadn't seen him yet, moved closer, pecking around in a patch of dry leaves for a snack. She was so preoccupied that he was able to creep forward a few steps, then a few more steps. The blackbird pulled up a worm.

"Now," thought Felis. "Jump—oops! No, wait."
First he had to figure out the direction the blackbird
would hop, and then plan his own jump accordingly
so that the bird wouldn't be able to get away. "To
the left," Felis thought. "She'll hop to the left."
There was no way he could miss.

He jumped and missed. The blackbird had not
hopped to the left. Screeching, she flew up into the
sky where no cat could possibly follow her.

"Stupid bird," said Felis, watching her. She landed
in a treetop and cawed down triumphantly.

"That's enough to give anyone a headache," Felis
grumbled. Whenever blackbirds saw him they cawed
that way. It was annoying. And the most bothersome
thing about it was that all the other birds would fly
away when they heard the shrieking. Angrily he hid
himself and waited for her to stop.

Then another voice joined in the calling of the
bird. Felis perked up his ears. He could not believe
what he was hearing.

"Stop that noise, you stupid bird! I can't hear a
thing around here. Felis! Felis!"

Felis thought he must be dreaming. No one in this
neighborhood ever called him by name.

"Felis! Felis!"

"Meeeoow!" Felis answered and ran toward the
voice.

And, indeed, it was one of his people. The man waited until Felis came running. Felis dropped onto his side with joy and murmured, "How nice that I have found you!"

"I found you," said the man.

"That's nice, too," Felis purred.

"And do you know why? Because I've been looking for you. For weeks I've been looking for you." The man scratched Felis in the way that only he could scratch. Then he took Felis in his arms. Felis rubbed his head into the man's neck and bit him gently on the chin.

The man held Felis tightly under his arm and began to walk away.

"Do we have to do this?" Felis asked.

"Now, hold still," said the man. He held Felis very tightly and then even more tightly as Felis began to struggle. Felis hated nothing in the world more than doing something his people wanted him to do, no matter how good their intentions. He began to scratch with his hind legs, and whenever he did that he was serious. Unfortunately, the man was a bit stronger than Felis.

And so they arrived at the car. Felis recognized it immediately. He was pushed inside, the door was closed, and the engine began its hideous roaring.

"Anything but this," Felis roared back. "I don't want to ride in a car."

"You're going to have to, cat."

"No!"

But no matter how hard Felis tried, the man would not give in. Felis could never figure it out, this thing with the car. At home they came running, whenever he wanted something. One little meow and they would bring food for him. Often he just sat looking at his plate and they knew what to do. But in the car, they were deaf even to his loudest cries.

"It won't take long," the man said, but a smart tomcat like Felis knew better than that.

But it really didn't take too long. The car came to a stop; the door opened. Felis jumped out into the fresh air.

Felis recognized everything inside the house, but it still seemed foreign to him. The smells had changed. Hardly any sign that he had lived there remained. But the woman greeted him the way she always had.

"How wonderful to have you back again," she said.

Felis purred, brushed against the leg of the table, and then turned to his plate. It was filled to the brim with sardines.

"I knew it," Felis rejoiced. Then he said nothing

more; he just ate. When he was done, he lay down on his old green pillow by the radiator and slept.

He would have slept much longer had they not stuck him in the car again and taken him to the vet.

"What is the meaning of this?" said Felis. "I'm not sick."

In the waiting room he grew quiet. As always, the smell of other animals frightened him. Even the people looked frightened. Felis trembled.

He didn't fully wake up until he was at home again. "The vet pricked me," he thought. "After that I don't remember a thing. I must have fallen asleep." His entire belly was sore, and he couldn't even lick at the pain because they had taped a bandage over it.

"Neutered," they said. A horrible word. They patted Felis on the head and said, "This is better for you. You won't have to run so far away because of the she-cats anymore. It's too dangerous out there. Big streets . . . the highway. Just think how easily a tomcat can get run over. We were afraid for you."

"Afraid!" thought Felis. "How ridiculous. As if I didn't know how to handle cars. After all, you can hear them coming from far away. Other toms might be stupid enough to run out in the street, but not me."

They wouldn't believe him. "What tomcat is going

to pay attention to cars when he is after a cat?" they said. "Now you won't have to worry about that anymore."

Felis was happy to be at home again, even though they had already stuck him in the car twice without asking. Home had its advantages. It was comfortable; you didn't have to worry about food, and you were loved.

"Aaaaaah," thought Felis as he stretched his paws out to their full length.

The man and the woman talked with him or left him alone as he wished, and the food was excellent. Felis was satisfied. He only disagreed with his people in regard to the black she-cat, the one who had smelled so different from the she-cats in his neighborhood. "When she calls me the next time," he thought, "I'll go again. They won't be able to stop me."

Finally the pain between his legs subsided. Lying around began to bore him. Felis hid behind the door frame and attacked anyone who walked by. He played cat and mouse with the man. And when the woman petted him, if she reached between his front paws he was gripped by such a wild impulse to hunt that he couldn't help grabbing her hand and kicking it. The woman turned into a dangerous enemy, and dangerous enemies had to be attacked from the side, bitten in the neck, and dragged down to the ground. Of course he didn't really bite her in the neck—only in the upper arm, the part that looked like the neck of a fat rat. The woman knew that he didn't really think she was a rat and that he would have bitten much differently had he been serious.

Then he barrelled up the steps.

"Do you hear our tomcat?" the man would ask the woman. "The weather is going to change."

"Nonsense," thought Felis. "I just want to go outside and you won't open the door."

Cloudy days gave way to the radiant sun of spring. Light streamed through the windows enticingly—but Felis still had to stay inside.

It was late morning and he was alone.

"What shall I do?" he mused. Felis did not do what he could not do. But since he mostly did what he could not keep from doing, he crept through the room and chased everything that was small enough to run away from him.

Felis felt a sudden need to use his box. Normally, he would have preferred to go in the yard, where he could leave his droppings in the flower beds or be-

tween the bushes and bury them with privacy. But the box served the same purpose. It was not, however, in its usual place. It was nowhere else to be found, either. It simply was not there.

"They must have put it outside and forgotten it," thought Felis.

But he needed it, and he needed it soon. Two o'clock, when the bus brought the woman home, was a long way off, so he would have to think of something else. "The best thing," it seemed to Felis, "would be to use the people-toilet. But that's impossible. It's too wet. How about the fluffy bath mat? Maybe I could bury it a bit. I'd better not. Then where? The floor? Disgusting. The wastepaper basket? Too narrow. The bookshelf? No." Felis finally decided on the bathtub.

"You did the right thing," the woman said at five past two. And she brought the forgotten box back into the house.

Chapter 10

"Hey, what's the meaning of this?" cried Felis.

For three days they had kept him inside the house. Now he had barely stepped out the front door to have a look around and what did he see? The spotted tom, sitting on his wall.

"What do you think you're doing here?"

The spotted tom turned his ears only slightly and

said, "That's exactly what I was just about to ask you."

Now that was a bit much. No sooner had Felis turned his back for a short while, tending to other matters, than other cats were settling into his place in the sun without permission.

"That is my wall," said Felis. "My house, my yard, my place in the sun, my wall."

"That *was* your wall," answered the spotted intruder.

But he didn't seem too sure of his own words, for Felis noticed how he pulled in his head and opened his mouth to a hiss that made no sound.

Felis turned away. "You idiot," he said. "I'm not even going to discuss it with you." Then he walked away stiffly and deliberately.

"Show-off!" hissed the other cat.

That was just fine with Felis. He smiled, for he who can smile is always the stronger one. Felis settled down by the steps, where the other tom could see him, and began to wash himself thoroughly. He washed his face, his shoulders, his stomach, his legs. He enjoyed teasing the intruder. When he got to his tail, the spotted one let out an annoyed hiss.

Felis turned briefly and said, "Why all the fuss? Can't you see I'm busy?" And with that, he walked away.

The truth was that Felis really did have a lot to do. He had to walk around the house, pace off all the paths in his yard, and snif at innumerable places. In doing so he soon discovered that every cat he had ever known had taken advantage of his absence. They seemed to have come and gone through his yard as they pleased. And he couldn't blame them— by smell alone even he wouldn't have known that he ever lived there. What's more, a she-cat who shared his tastes must have moved into the neighborhood. More than once, she had lain down on all of his favorite plants. It was important that he meet this cat very soon. But first he had to bring some order back to his territory.

Felis was not satisfied until he had left behind traces of his scent everywhere. After he did this, he sharpened his claws on the apple tree and was finally ready to lie in the sun—which was hanging high in the sky, just waiting to warm his fur. He headed for his favorite sunbathing wall, determined to chase away any cat who dared be in that spot. "If the spotted tom doesn't know his place," Felis thought to himself, "then I'll just have to get tough."

In passing, Felis sniffed at the plants. The sage and the catnip were not yet in bloom. But the smell of morning glories already filled the air. With the sweet scent of blossoms in his nose, he strolled on until he

got to the steps. From there he peeked around the corner at his wall. The spotted tom must have expected Felis to come back, because he had left. "So there," said Felis. Then he looked around, jumped onto the wall, and yawned.

When the sun had climbed even higher in the sky, Felis heard someone coming down the path. Instantly he was wide awake. The white tom was strolling down the path as if it were his own. He sniffed at the post and looked around, rather puzzled. When he spotted Felis, he looked visibly uneasy.

"I had no idea you were back," he mumbled.

Felis didn't trust him. "I suppose you're here to lie on my wall," he hissed.

"Don't worry, don't worry," the white cat replied. "Nobody wants to lie on your wall." He sat down on the warm stones and purred.

Felis believed this, but he didn't curl up on his paws again until the white tom had left.

It was the kind of day Felis liked best—no breeze and sunny. A perfect day for dozing and listening. But on this day, Felis was destined to find no rest. No sooner had he lowered his head than the next visitor appeared.

"Oh, no," Felis sighed. "Not again." It was the gray tom.

The gray trotted purposefully toward the wall, never suspecting anyone else's presence.

Felis sat up.

Startled, the gray tom stopped midstride. But then he made a move to chase Felis away. Half ready to fall, half ready to attack, the gray rose onto his hind legs.

"If you want a fight," Felis said, "you can have one."

This wall belonged to him and he was prepared to defend it. Plus, being higher than his opponent, he had the more favorable position for fighting. He glared down angrily at the gray tomcat.

"Get lost!" he growled.

The gray tom hissed once more, then turned away.

"What a day," Felis thought wearily as he settled back on the wall. "It's as if all these guys had gotten together and decided, 'Let's annoy Felis today.' Well, nobody else had better try it."

But the gray was not to be his last visitor. As evening fell and Felis had settled under the rhododendron to listen to the beetles rustling, a she-cat entered the yard. "That must be the new cat," he thought. She was slender and black, with white feet. She came out of the bushes and ran across the

grass—carefully, it seemed to Felis, but purposefully. "She obviously can't see me," he thought. "Soon enough she'll find out who I am."

"Hey!" he called. And again, "Hey!"

The second call was unnecessary. Already the she-cat had stopped still and was peering nervously in Felis' direction.

He came out from under the bush, took a few steps, and sat down.

The new cat regained her poise. She pretended not to notice Felis at all. She sat down and gazed around the yard. Felis said nothing; he simply stood up and raised his hackles. This was enough for the she-cat; she became quite nervous.

Felis approached her menacingly. "I've had enough," he said.

For a moment it seemed that the cat was going to jump at him. But instead she walked away.

"Good plan," said Felis. "I'm glad you know your place."

Chapter 11

The new she-cat lived next door, in a house where formerly only people had lived.

"Let's see," Felis thought the very next morning. "Let's see how she spends her time."

The she-cat was sitting peacefully on the steps to her house when Felis approached.

The moment she saw him, she rose to her feet and froze. As she looked him over, her tail swayed back and forth. And when Felis came closer, she lifted her rear end slightly.

"I don't know what you think you're trying to prove," said Felis. The she-cat had no right to this yard, in his opinion. It ought to remain no-cat's land, where he could move as freely as he wanted, just as he always had.

The she-cat lowered her head and braced her hind legs for a jump.

"Oh, stop making such a fuss," said Felis and walked on.

The she-cat flattened her ears so closely to her head that you couldn't even see them anymore. She opened her eyes wide and raised her front paw to take a swipe at him. It was a terrible sight to behold, this she-cat with the bared teeth.

"How ridiculous," Felis grumbled, retreating a few steps. "She's really serious about this."

With a wild growl, the she-cat started coming toward him, hissing anxiously.

This was finally too much for Felis. There was no telling what she might do. "I might as well go back home," he thought.

Once his anger had subsided, Felis made a tour of his own yard to be sure that everything was in order.

He decided to spend the rest of the morning in the meadow by the hill. "I'll walk for fifteen minutes," he thought, "and then maybe I'll catch myself a mouse. That would be just the thing for me right now."

The path led through the hole in the fence and off to the right through the bushes. But when Felis turned right, he saw the gray tom sitting there, deep in thought. And since Felis knew better than to disturb a thinking cat, he headed to the left. But the left-hand path didn't go to the sloping meadow; it led to the farm, and Felis never went to the farm at this time of day.

As he walked along, Felis grew more and more disgruntled. Why should he have to change his habits just because he had been away for a few weeks? He looked back to the right once more, but couldn't figure out what to do.

So Felis sat down, began washing himself, and then finally decided to go back home.

But Felis still wasn't in the mood for a quiet morning; he had had enough lying around. Three days in the house were more than enough, and now it was time for something to happen. He swatted at a fly. "*Bzzzzz, bzzzzz.*" It was a brave fly, one of those

shimmering, fat flies that he could never scare. Humming loudly, it circled Felis' nose, angling down to land. Felis ducked.

"*Bzzzzz, bzzzzz,*" said the fly.

"Forget about it," Felis replied. "You're too small for me."

Felis actually knew that he couldn't catch the fly. It seemed to realize this, too. It buzzed away. "I need bigger excitement than this," Felis thought. "Maybe that little brown bird that just landed on the birdbath." But no sooner had Felis taken two careful steps forward than the bird fluttered away. Felis followed it with his eyes. "Birds are mean," he thought. "First they tease you and then they fly away. It's not fair."

At that moment he heard something. His right ear registered a very soft, high-pitched peeping from the opposite corner of the yard. Now he knew how to occupy himself. He crouched and advanced, briefly going under cover until the peeping started again, and then crept on. Then he saw it. A dry leaf was moving and a mouse just had to be under it.

Although Felis had enough time, he knew he couldn't make any mistakes. "Just a little bit farther," he coached himself, "without a sound, because mice have sensitive ears. Wait, watch, and pounce."

At that very moment the mouse turned and stared at him. Felis started back a tiny bit. He knew that mice can bite. Not that he was really afraid. This was a mouse and not a rat. But since one always has to be prepared for the worst, it was time to be extra careful.

Had the mouse seen him?

Fortunately, mice don't have very good eyesight. Felis remained completely still. Not a hair on his body moved, not even the tip of his tail. No, it couldn't possibly have seen him. It looked away again and scurried a few steps farther.

"Just a little longer, and then he's mine," thought Felis. "At just the right moment, I'm going to shoot forward and take my prize."

Felis pounced. He got it. He held it and shook it until it stopped moving. But it couldn't possibly be dead yet. Felis put the mouse back on the ground, and a minute later it ran away and he had to chase it all over again. Whenever he caught it, he let it go. His heart was pounding and every muscle in his body twitched with excitement. Only then did he bite the mouse. He hopped around the dead mouse a few times, poking it and pushing at it. Then he grew calmer.

"Too bad," he thought. "Now I'm bored again."

The day he killed his first mouse, Felis had been completely surprised when the animal had stopped moving. It had taken him a moment to understand what he had done. Only much later did he realize that a mouse you could no longer play with changed into something else—something you could eat. Actually, his mother had shown him that.

Felis touched his prey with his paw, figuring out which was the front end, then carried it off to a sheltered spot to eat it. He looked it over, sniffed at it, and finally admitted, "To be honest, the food on my plate tastes better than this."

And so Felis decided not to eat the mouse. Instead he brought it into the kitchen and laid it on the floor.

"Oh my goodness," said the woman.

Felis looked up at her questioningly.

"Don't worry," she said, trying to calm down. "You did very well. You are a good hunter, really; a very good hunter."

Felis turned away. This was hardly news to him. He had brought her the mouse so that he could teach her what you are supposed to do with mice, just like his mother had taught him. He also knew that in the human mind, things to eat belonged in the kitchen.

"A mouse," she repeated. Felis thought he detected a trace of disgust in her voice.

Felis knew a great deal about humans. He knew when they were feeling suspicious. Their eyes grew long and slanted. In this respect they were like cats. Although his people walked only on their hind legs and acted differently in other ways, Felis was convinced that he could count them among the four-legged animals. And he believed that anything on four legs could be treated as another cat, whether it was big or small. There were exceptions to this rule, he had learned: dogs, who strangely enough wagged their tails when they were being friendly, and also the very smallest of the other four-legged animals (because they ran away, and anything that runs away must be chased).

"Of course it's a mouse!" he told the woman in a friendly voice. "Not a fly, and not a rat, but a mouse."

This mouse was his contribution to the household. But the woman just stared at it as if she had no idea what to do with it, no idea at all. She carried the mouse by the tail out into the yard without even smelling it. This was the dumbest thing she could possibly have done.

"People," thought Felis. "They still have a lot to

learn." He knew that he would have to be patient and carry quite a few more mice into the house before he could teach them what it was all about.

Chapter 12

A few days later he happened to catch the new she-cat sitting in his place in the sun. She brushed over her left ear with her front paw a few times and then licked her fur clean. It wasn't until she had brushed her right ear as well that Felis took a step forward. She must have been very preoccupied, because even this escaped her attention.

Usually when he saw her, she was perched on a high place, looking down distrustfully on everything below. And even though the one who sits above is always the stronger one, she didn't look so strong. She looked worried, even up there on top of his wall.

Felis didn't like the fact that someone could look down at him. Especially in his own yard.

"Come down from there," he said.

She heard exactly what he said but she did not budge. And when he tried to jump up onto the wall, she hissed at him.

"You must be crazy," Felis exclaimed, but he let her be. "If that's your idea of fun, fine," he thought.

He walked around the house and lay down on a sandy spot next to a big oak tree.

It didn't take long before he heard soft footsteps. The she-cat made a small detour around him, casting him a quick glance that was not exactly friendly but also not hostile. He didn't return her glance. He knew you should never tease someone who's nervous. Only after she was beyond him did he look her way.

When he was outside making his rounds that night, Felis heard the clatter of a trash-can lid falling to the ground, somewhere down the block. Curious, he trotted out to investigate and barely caught sight of a cat dashing away. "That has to be the new cat," he thought, and hid behind a tree to watch. When all remained quiet for a while, the she-cat cautiously returned and jumped back onto the edge of the trash can. Effortlessly maintaining her balance, she fished something out of it. Felis could not make out what it was, but in any case the she-cat gobbled it up as soon as she jumped to the ground.

"Poor cat," he thought. "She doesn't get enough to eat."

Noticing Felis, the new cat politely lifted her tail and said, "There's still a bit left."

"I'm not hungry, thanks."

"That doesn't matter," she said. "You should always eat whenever you get the chance."

But then a window opened up above. Water poured down over the cats.

"How nasty can you get?" said Felis, when they had settled under the bushes to lick themselves dry.

"What do you expect?" she said. "People."

"That's not the way things usually are around here," said Felis. "But we don't usually get into the trash cans, either."

The cat looked at him with a puzzled expression on her face. "You are all quite strange here," she said. "I think I'll go back home soon."

Two days passed before he saw her again. She was standing on top of his birdbath, drinking. It was night. The moonlight shone through the clouds, so he recognized her easily. At a polite distance he stopped and said, "Good evening, neighbor. Are you still thinking of leaving? It seems to me you haven't been here very long."

"No," she said. "You haven't either."

"Oh, yes, I have," said Felis. "Actually, I've almost always been here."

She looked at him with surprise.

"It's a peculiar neighborhood," she finally replied. "Hardly any water. So many yards. Streets. Cars. But I do like the yards."

Now it was Felis' turn to look surprised, because he didn't find the neighborhood peculiar at all. It seemed completely normal to him. After a short silence he said, "May I inquire who you are?"

She said nothing, so he went a little closer and sniffed at her. She let him walk all the way around her and sniff; then she did the same to him. They both sat down.

In the house next door a window opened.

They heard a worried voice. "Venezia! Venezia!"

This wasn't the first time that Felis had heard that call.

"He means me," said the cat. "The man I live with. He wants me to come home."

"Hmmmmm," said Felis.

"But I'm not going to go."

"Of course not," said Felis. "I only go home when I want to, also—never when they tell me to come. And Venezia—my name's Felis."

The two cats spoke very politely to each other. They chose their words carefully. First of all, you're never sure in the beginning which words to use with a cat you don't know well. Secondly, talkativeness never makes a good impression. And thirdly, it's not always easy to think of something to say.

"You have very good water out here," Venezia finally said. "In your birdbath, I mean."

Felis wasn't sure of an appropriate response. "Hmmmm." he said.

"I'm glad that I can drink here in your yard."

Felis was silent for a while. Then he said, "Hmmmm."

"In our house the water smells disgusting."

"It does in our house, too," he said. "Heaven only knows what people put in their water to make it smell that way."

"Chlorine," said Venezia. "Fluoride. Terrible stuff. It stinks. We don't have that where I come from."

This left Felis truly speechless. She had used words he had never heard before.

"You don't have very much water around here anyway, if I may say so," Venezia continued. "Where I come from, water flows almost everywhere between the houses."

"Water!" said Felis. "Disgusting."

"You just have to watch out. But it smells good. Of course there are also alleys and squares and trash bags and garbage bins. You have to live somehow."

Venezia thought of the countless cats that roamed her neighborhood in search of something to eat. During the warmer seasons, when lots of people were around, the cats ate their fill. The winters were harder. You fought with the other cats and then made up again. You raised your children. You had friends.

"I think I might go back home soon," said Venezia.

Chapter 13

Felis, who in the past had felt free to cut through the yard next door, now took the path across the street. He didn't want to provoke any arguments with his new neighbor, especially since they were almost getting along.

Venezia was crouching on a ledge above the street, looking scared to death, when Felis walked by.

"A car just missed me by a whisker," she gasped.

"Not to worry," said Felis. "Anything that makes so much noise while hunting can't be too dangerous."

"I just can't get used to it," said Venezia. "We don't have cars where I live. And what's worse, cars stink. I'll have to go back home soon."

But that evening she was still there. Felis met her on his way to the hazel bush.

"It's good to see you," said Venezia. "At least I can talk to you. The others only give me trouble."

"Trouble?" asked Felis.

"Where I live, cats know how to get along with each other."

"They do here, too. You'll see."

In the entire neighborhood, there wasn't one she-cat or tomcat that Felis didn't know. They had all fought and sniffed each other and gathered together on the sloping meadow at night. They had long ago determined who was the strongest, who was the most courageous, and even who was the most stubborn. Among the tomcats in particular, everything had its order. Each tomcat knew just how far he could push another at any given moment, just by one quick glance. A tom like the gray tiger could hiss and spit and flatten his ears and nobody would be frightened.

101

At most, they would do him the favor of avoiding him, since he took everything so seriously. If, however, the white tom, who was clearly ranked first among them, so much as looked askance, they knew better than to pick a fight with him.

When two cats' paths crossed, it was clear who had the right of way. The tom with the higher ranking went first—that was the rule. A nice rule, but it was rarely followed because whoever reached the crossing first usually went on ahead. Even the white tom wasn't particularly bothered when that happened. And everyone respected the property borders around the houses. This, again, wasn't too much of a hassle, because the boundaries only mattered when the owner was home. And what cat is stupid enough to sit in his yard all day long?

So they were able to live together. When differences of opinion arose from time to time, they were usually settled without a fight. All of the toms stated their opinions to one another and stated them clearly—but they tried not to squabble. Any squabble involves a risk.

Venezia had arrived and started to cross other cats' yards, run across the meadow, hunt in other cats' favorite spots, and, most regrettably, defend her own yard (which had been open to all). Now a certain uneasiness filled their society. She was new. She was

102

different. Nobody trusted her. Every she-cat and every tom who met her tried to sniff her, and when she did not let them, they attacked her. She defended herself as best she could. But she rarely had a quiet moment—except when she was with Felis.

Even between the established cats, peace no longer prevailed. There was a constant, suspicious bickering and hissing among the friends who had gotten along so well before.

The night gatherings were no longer relaxing and social. They were all too excited. Instead of gossiping, they growled. Old rivalries sprang up anew. The she-cat with the brown ears could no longer tolerate the arrogant expression on the white tom's face. She attacked him without notice and chased him away. The gray tom scratched up the spotted one's face. Even Felis attacked the she-cat with black paws when she tried to cut through his yard.

Felis came home with scratch wounds.

"To the vet?" asked the man.

"Anything but that," said Felis, although he knew no one would listen to him.

Fortunately the woman said, "Maybe we should wait."

"What a wonderful idea." Felis was relieved.

103

"It doesn't seem to be too bad. He just needs some rest."

She fluffed up his pillow. When Felis went over to the door and looked up at the handle, she picked him up and took him to his pillow. As if he had ever lain down where someone else had wanted him to.

"Would you please open the door now?" he said.

When nothing happened, Felis looked away. Out of sight out of mind, as people said. What nonsense. Felis was convinced that even people could think about something they could not see. Looking away doesn't mean that you can't see anything. Even if you can't see something, you notice it instantly when it moves. And once it moves, everything changes.

"Oh, all right," said the woman. "If you're going to be stubborn about it."

One Wednesday morning, Felis heard a clattering sound. A clattering and a rustling. He walked down the street until the smell of fish reached his nostrils.

Venezia was sitting in front of a house, pawing through a pile of garbage. A torn plastic bag lay beside her.

"That smells good," said Felis. He helped her pull out even more trash until they finally found the fish. It seemed to be fresh.

But they never had a chance to eat it. A woman came running out of the house, waving a broom and shouting, "You pesky little beasts! Street cats! You ought to be locked up!"

Then she swept everything together and into a new black bag.

"What a waste of good fish," Venezia complained.

When the woman had gone into the house, the cat with the brown ears appeared, apparently lured by the delicious lingering smell. As soon as she noticed Venezia, she twisted her face into a threatening grimace. Venezia reacted with lightning speed. She jumped—to surprise her attacker and to gain enough time to dash away. The cat with the brown ears screeched and ran after her.

Felis decided that this was the perfect opportunity to make his exit. He ambled back home and stretched out under the rhododendron for a nap.

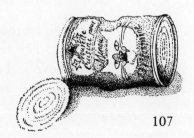

Chapter 14

The evenings grew warmer. One night, when the moon was shining overhead, Felis slipped through the bushes to the house next door. "I'll just see what she's up to," he thought as he looked around the corner.

Venezia was sitting on the steps. The moment she saw him she rose to her feet and turned her ears toward him inquisitively. Felis stopped at a polite distance. She didn't look as though she wanted to chase him away. Her nostrils twitched slightly. But that was all.

"A pleasant evening," Felis purred reassuringly. "May I visit with you?"

Her expression grew much friendlier, indeed. "Come in, come in," she said. "Because it's you."

With slightly stiff legs, she approached him and greeted him with a touch on the nose. She wasn't afraid anymore. At least not of him.

But when a woman inside the house came to the back door, Venezia flattened herself against the wall.

"What's the matter?" said Felis. "I know that woman. It can't be that bad living with her—she likes cats."

"So she likes cats," said Venezia. "So what? Does that mean I have to like her?"

"I guess that's up to you," Felis replied.

He had liked people ever since he was a little kitten. Before he had even been able to see anything, he had heard their voices and felt their hands. "I have always thought of people," he said, "as big cats."

"You've got to be kidding," Venezia grunted. "That's enough to make a mouse laugh. Next time you'll be saying that cats are like little people."

"Why not?" said Felis bravely. "I think people are very much like cats. But not so much that you always have to treat them like cats. That's the nice thing about them. You purr; they feed you. You lie down on your back; they scratch your stomach. No one's done that for me since I left my mother. People have a feeling for friendship, I think."

"You must be crazy," Venezia said, petulantly. She had spent her entire life with other cats and had always been taught to avoid people. This was the first time that she had even lived in a human's house. Her human had found her, brought her home, fed her, taken her in his arms, stuck her in a car again, and dragged her to the vet. "Without even asking me," she said. "People never ask. And what's worse is that he always wants to pet me."

"I like being petted," said Felis.

"I don't," she said. "Sometimes I even have to hiss at him. The only thing I like about him is that he's generous with food. But does that mean I have to sit around the house all day long? He'd prefer to lock me up day and night, you know. Not me, I told him. I figured out right away how to open the door. I just wait until he falls asleep and then out I go."

"You do that yourself?" Felis laughed. "That's too much of a nuisance for me. I let them open the door for me. My people think that I'm too dumb to open the door. Are they ever wrong about that! I just don't want to. But I let them think so. They like doing me the favor. It's good for our friendship."

"Friendship?" said Venezia. "How can you have a friendship with someone who likes to keep you prisoner? Whenever I want to go out at night, he says no. He's probably afraid that I'll never come back. And someday I won't."

"You mean you'll just run away?" asked Felis. "That's a great idea." Felis was tired of sitting around. He pretended to take a swing at her, then raised his tail like a squirrel and bounded away. "You can't catch me!"

"Want to bet?" she cried, immediately dashing after him. He hadn't even reached his yard before she tackled him and knocked him down.

"Oh, no, you don't," said Felis. "That's no way to act with me." He turned around and chased her. They laughed and hissed and their game grew wilder and wilder.

"Quiet!" someone shouted out of a window.

"Quiet yourself!" Venezia cried and scampered up the nearest tree.

Felis followed in a flash.

He perched himself on the highest branch and looked around. Venezia was sitting one branch below him, looking around as well. The ground was very far below them.

"Where to now?" she said.

"Down, I would say," Felis replied uneasily. "We certainly can't go farther up."

"And how?"

"Jump, I'd say."

"Too far up."

"On the contrary," said Felis. "Too far down."

Venezia slid a little farther out on her branch and repeated, "Too far up."

Felis bent over and tried, without success, to climb down at least one branch. "Too far down, I'd say."

"Too far up!" she called to him, running out of patience. "And this stupid tree doesn't have enough branches."

"I'll agree with you there. Any respectable tree has ten times as many branches as this one."

The tree had a further disadvantage. It stood right next to the house with the open window where the lady still stood yelling.

"Quiet!" the voice shouted directly into their ears.

"If you want peace and quiet, then you shouldn't make so much noise," Venezia screeched back.

They sat in the tree and laughed. Only after they had a good laugh did they begin their descent. Backwards. Grip with the claws, slide a bit, grip again, slide. It was a long and tiring process.

When they had finally arrived safely on the

ground, they smoothed down their fur and sat down. Whenever Felis wrapped his tail around himself, he always rolled it from the left to the right, while Venezia always rolled hers from the right to the left. Every now and then they blinked, their eyes half-closed. And so they sat, contentedly breathing in the warm night air.

Felis was silent. Anyone who sits and is silent has a secret, even if he or she doesn't know it. Sooner or later it will emerge. Silence is like an invisible light that shines on secrets. But not just any silence. It has to be a silence that someone is listening to.

When two cats sit in the moonlight and are silent together, it means they are also listening. And that means that they must understand each other very, very well.

Venezia and Felis had been sitting for quite some time before she rose and licked his neck. When she had finished, she sat down and looked away.

Felis knew it was his turn. He obediently went over to her and returned the favor.

The moon disappeared. It grew darker.

"I'm glad that you're here," she said. "The other cats don't like me."

"Just wait," said Felis. "They don't know you yet. Soon they'll like you, too."

113

Chapter 15

Little patches of light bounced across the ground beneath the hazel bush while the wind rustled through the leaves.

"You'd better watch out!" said Felis. "I can catch anything that moves, dead or alive!"

The patches of light didn't dare to move. Only a dry leaf that had not heard him rustled in the wind. Felis crept a few steps forward and pressed himself against the ground. As soon as the leaf began moving again, he sprang, grabbed it, and fell onto his side,

116

holding it. The leaf almost seemed to drag him to the ground. "Just wait," said Felis, "I'll show you a thing or two." The leaf did its best to defend itself, but Felis held on with all his might, kicking with his hind feet until the leaf lost consciousness.

Felis freed his prey, but it no longer moved. What was left of it lay on the ground, motionless. "Well, you started it," Felis said as he rose to his feet and shook himself. With his eyes and ears alert, he waited for whatever would next have the nerve to cross his path.

The leaf, having had a moment's rest, hopped on, catching a gust of wind.

"What!" cried Felis. "You're not dead after all? Well, you'll regret that."

The leaf took a leap.

Felis bounded after it, his tail curled like a question mark. Then he jumped into the air and ran on, with wild pounces every so often at the tantalizing leaf.

He saw Venezia lying on the wall.

Felis kept running toward her at full speed and then braked with all his might to impress her. And he would have succeeded, if only she had opened her eyes. As a joke, he hid himself and looked up expectantly.

Her eyes remained closed. He jumped onto the wall.

"Are you asleep?" he asked.

Gently he brushed his nose against her face.

"Hey!"

"Hey?" Felis lay down beside her with one paw on her fur. "I was asking you whether you were asleep."

"Of course I'm asleep."

"Then why didn't you say so right away?"

"Thanks for reminding me," she said.

"Hmmmmm?"

"I think today is Wednesday."

"Of course today is Wednesday."

"So," said Venezia, "what are we waiting for?"

Felis had no idea what she meant.

"Wednesdays," she said. "That's when they put the garbage out."

"Who?"

"Just come on. No time for sleep!" She jumped up. "Let's see what we can find."

They had already rummaged through three bags without finding anything when Venezia perked up her ears. She heard a door, then loud footsteps. They scrambled away just in time.

When they arrived home once again, it started to rain.

"What a bother."

118

The doors were all shut and Felis knew no one was home.

"Nobody's at my house, either," she said. "Around here," she added after a while, "you can't do anything without humans' getting in the way. Also the other cats. And it's raining. I've had enough. What are we waiting for? Let's get going."

Felis looked around indecisively.

"I'll lead," she said. "It can't be very far. Just a stone's throw away."

"Now?"

"When else?"

"When it's stopped raining. This is hardly the weather for emigrating."

Venezia sighed. "You might be right. This weather is disgusting."

"It's dry out back, under the hedge. That's where I always go when it rains."

"I know," she said.

They had to crawl through a narrow hole between the branches and the ground. Venezia waited. "After you, please."

That's what Felis liked best about her, the polite manners of an experienced street cat. Once they were under the bush, there was plenty of room. Felis licked her fur where it had gotten wet. When he was finished he said, "Now it's my turn."

119

Venezia obliged.

Then they lay still and listened to the raindrops.

It is not the custom among cats to ask each other questions. There is a reason for this. Cats are born knowing what they need to know to survive. But since nothing ever stays the same, cats also have to learn new things. For this they use their eyes, noses, ears, and whiskers. Anyone who thinks cats cannot find out everything they need to know with these tools is both right and wrong. Anything a cat cannot find out in this manner is probably not worth knowing.

So if a cat asks another cat a question, it's hardly a big deal—as long as the other cat doesn't know the answer, either. If the other cat does know the answer, then you've got a problem. Because then that cat would be showing that he knows more than the cat who asked, which would mean the cat who asked knows less, and no cat can easily admit that. That's why a cat who has just been asked a question will look around for a long time and say nothing, in the hope that the one who asked the question will forget about it. And if a cat looks around long enough, then something else is bound to prove distracting. A flea could bite. Or a fly could buzz by. A dog could bark. A small brown bird might come for a drink. And

then there are always the general rustling sounds.

There are at least a thousand reasons to forget that a question has been asked.

"I would like to ask you something," said Venezia. "May I?"

Felis was startled.

"And you have to answer."

Felis looked at his paws. Then he lifted an ear to where a bird was chirping. Venezia persisted.

"Where are your rats?"

"What kind of rats?"

"Black ones, gray ones, brown ones—any kind."

Disgusted, Felis pawed the ground with his hind paws. "Brown rats. How repulsive."

"I don't care what they look like. Where are they?"

"I don't think we have any rats here."

"That's too bad."

Felis said nothing. He was glad. He hated rats. They were too dangerous for him.

"Rats taste good."

"Maybe. But you have to catch them first."

"Exactly," she said. "I don't want to say anything against your neighborhood. But if there were rats around, I'd like it much better. There really isn't anything exciting to hunt here, is there?"

This had never occurred to Felis.

"There are plenty of rats where I'm from," she continued. "You really have to prove yourself there."

Felis wasn't sure if he could prove himself against a rat. He watched a leaf fall and said nothing. His mother had caught rats. When she brought them back home, she loudly growled, "Rat!" The word alone sounded threatening, although just to be safe she only brought home dead rats. He had always preferred the word *mouse* because it sounded as though you could have fun with it.

"I prefer mice." After a pause, he added, "There are supposed to be rats in the city. The white tom told us about them. But it's far away."

"That doesn't matter. I've got stamina."

"Well, the white tom said that it's dangerous, too. The city is so full of cars you can hardly walk anywhere."

"No," she said, looking to the side and blinking. "He must have made that up. I've always thought he was an exaggerator."

"He lived there," said Felis.

"So did I," said Venezia. "For two years. And the whole time I didn't see a single car. Only boats."

Felis scratched himself. "She is a city cat," he thought. "So she must know."

Chapter 16

"It's after two," said Felis at five past two. He had heard footsteps on the street and ran around the yard to the front.

"Horrid weather," said the woman as she unlocked the door.

Felis rubbed his wet fur against her legs. He was the first to dash into the dry house—straight into the kitchen.

"It's not time to eat yet," said the woman.

"I know."

He chewed on a few dry scraps that were left over from breakfast while the woman rustled a newspaper in the living room. He followed the rustling sound, sat down in front of the sofa between the two legs that stuck out from under the paper, and let out a nice full *meow*. Not *mrrr* or *mmm-ow*, but *meow*, the way he said it to his people when he had a particular wish. Felis would never have addressed another cat with a full *meow*. That language is not spoken among his kind.

The woman understood. She put aside the newspaper so he could jump onto her lap. He offered her his nose to sniff, then his hindquarters, and then he lay down in such a way that he could gently knead her stomach. She liked that, and Felis liked it so much that he purred louder and louder until he forgot about everything else. It almost seemed as if the woman began to purr, too, because purring is contagious.

Suddenly Felis realized that he had fallen asleep. Startled, he jumped up and looked around. He wasn't the type to sleep on laps. He decided to move to the newspaper that was lying in front of the sofa. Settling down onto it, he fell asleep almost before its pages stopped rustling.

As he let himself fall asleep, Felis felt as if he were falling into a cave that was very dark but smelled wonderfully of sweet flowers and catnip.

Felis sniffed and sniffed. He couldn't get enough of the sweetness. In the distance, where the cave grew even darker, he saw two tiny eyes flashing. Felis forgot all the pleasant smells and took cover. The eyes belonged to an animal that scampered across the ground fearlessly. It was small, like a mouse, and it came closer and closer. Felis watched. He didn't pounce until the mouse tried to run away. And then he missed.

"That was a mistake," he thought. But what difference did it make? He knew that mistakes are made so that you can do better the next time.

The mouse returned, unafraid. Felis jumped a second time. But even on his third try he failed to catch it.

"Felis, Felis," he said to himself. "This is useless."

What to do?

Wait.

To be on the safe side, Felis watched the animal out of the corner of his eye. Something about it bothered him. It was clear that this wasn't any ordinary mouse. Now and then this animal that was not a mouse sat down and scratched itself. And every time it scratched itself, it grew a little bit bigger. Then it gave Felis a mean look and scratched itself again.

"That's enough," said Felis. "You stop that."

The creature really wasn't a mouse anymore; it was a rat—a terrifying, ugly brown rat. And it kept on growing.

"Rat!" Felis cried.

Something had to be done. He didn't even have time to fluff up his tail as he whipped it from side to side. He jumped.

The rat hadn't expected this. At the very last moment, it turned to avoid the crash. But Felis had jumped from the side and twisted in the air, falling on the rat so it toppled over. It was a strong rat, and it freed itself immediately from Felis' neckhold to strike him back. As it bit and scratched, the rat seemed to grow even bigger.

Felis had to finish off this beast before it grew to his own size. But he also had to be careful to keep an escape route clear in case of emergency.

He lay on his side and pulled in his head to avoid the rat's bite, but still he held it firmly, kicking it with his hind legs. The rat defended itself in vain. Its movements grew weaker. At that point Felis started biting.

He had done it. The rat was dead. Felis jumped up in the air and wriggled with joy.

"Felis, Felis," said the rat.

But it spoke with a human voice. And Felis felt a human hand on his back. The newspapers beneath him rustled. He opened his eyes.

"Too bad," he thought. "It was all just a dream."

At that very moment, he heard the five o'clock bus. "Should I go to the door? Greet the man? No, first I'll wake up properly and clean my fur."

A cat's lick is a very thorough way to wash, and

Felis never missed a single spot. Like everything that is important, good washing takes time. After he had cleaned himself all over, Felis began again with his ears.

When the man walked through the door, he said, "Ah, it's going to rain. The cat is washing himself behind the ears."

"Is that supposed to be some kind of a joke?" Felis muttered "It's already raining, isn't it?"

Perhaps it had stopped.

Felis asked to have the door opened. He stepped outside, but quickly came back in. Of course it was still raining. It was colder than he had thought, too. He lay down in the doorway so that he might examine the situation thoroughly.

"Hey, Slit Ear," the man said. "Move. The door won't shut."

"No," said Felis. "It's not supposed to."

The weather, he decided, was a bit much. "What do you think of it?" he asked the man.

"Horrid," said the man. "I wouldn't go out."

"I'm going, then," said Felis.

But he didn't move, he stayed put and listened. Anyone who sits and listens is not impatient.

Then the woman came and took him in her arms. That was all right. What was not all right was that she stuck him in the carrier.

130

"What's the meaning of this?" he cried in surprise. "I knew it," he added. "I should have gone out after all. Then you wouldn't have found me."

The woman said the tiger-striped cat had died of a virus. She had lost her sense of smell, stopped eating, and had grown weaker and weaker. The long and the short of it was that they had to take Felis to the vet to be vaccinated.

Vaccinated!

"We have to, so you don't get sick."

"I don't get sick. Ever. Can't you see?"

A horrible day. First the rain, and now this.

At the vet's he was placed, as usual, on a table where other animals had been put before him. A hand grabbed him by the neck so he couldn't move. And then there was the smell of fear that he hated so much. He would have liked to simply hold his breath. Off to one side, he faintly heard the woman's soothing voice. But his heart was pounding so loudly that he could barely hear anything at all. Then a prick in his side. And another prick.

This was too much.

"You fat rat of a veterinarian," thought Felis. "You'd better watch out."

Without warning, Felis swung with outstretched claws at the hand gripping his side and prepared to jump down. But he didn't make it. The hand was faster. Its grip tightened. Then he gathered all his strength and tore away. With sheer desperation, Felis jumped at the vet's face and bit him.

The vet recoiled. Felis seized the opportunity to escape. He barricaded himself under the cabinet and wouldn't let anyone near him.

This worked until a man came through the door with a dog. The dog bared his teeth and growled. But not even this could frighten Felis. He saw nothing but the open door and dashed out.

When they were finally home again, Felis lay down on his green pillow, exhausted.

The man shook his head. "Felis, Felis. That was not very nice and you know it."

"Maybe not," said Felis. "But I really showed him this time. He won't touch me again."

Chapter 17

"Felis! Felis!"

Felis opened his eyes and yawned. "Seven o'clock already?" he thought. "I must have overslept."

"Felis! Felis!"

Felis hated to yawn quickly. When he yawned, he yawned properly. He still needed to stretch, too. This he also did very thoroughly, for why bother to stretch at all if you don't do it thoroughly? Felis even stretched the top of his tail. Then he ran into the house.

Felis loved lengthy greetings and would not have been satisfied with mumbling a brief good morning on his way into the kitchen. The woman knew this, and sat down beside him on the floor. While he purred, she said all his favorite things so that he would purr even louder and press his head into her hand. He was so full of joy that he didn't even listen very carefully. Only after enough of that did she say the words that he liked to hear most of all, especially when he was hungry: Time to eat. Felis rose to his feet and led the way into the kitchen.

Around the corner, to the plate, crouch down, sniff, and eat; this was the proper sequence. But this time he got only as far as the sniffing. His plate did not smell good. "Where in the world did you find this stuff?" he asked, insulted. "Is it left over from yesterday?" Scornfully he flung his tail to one side and began to paw with hind legs as if he were burying something disgusting. Then he took three steps back, sat down, and looked at the woman without saying another word.

"What's wrong?" she asked, staring at him with wide green eyes.

At times she seemed to forget that you're not supposed to stare. Particularly at friends. Only if you're afraid or have bad intentions. But she wasn't afraid, and she certainly didn't have any bad intentions. She must be making a mistake.

Felis squinted his eyes a bit and politely turned his head to the side.

Then he said, quietly, "Could you please give me something decent to eat?"

"I don't understand what you're grumbling about," she said.

Felis remained silent. If she didn't know herself, then she would take his efforts to explain to mean nothing more than *meow*. What's more, she had a nose of her own.

Felis continued to wait while she clattered around with the dishes overhead.

"*Mow*," he said quietly.

"*Mooooow!*" She clattered on without even moving her ears. It was as if they had grown flat to her head. Maybe humans would understand more if they could move their ears. But he never mentioned this to them because he was afraid it would embarrass them.

Felis finally gave up and went into the living room. He sat down in front of the sofa. The question was whether or not to actually lie down. Maybe wash first and then lie down? Or not lie down at all and go outside? Or wash first and then go outside? Or first one and then the other or first the other and then the one?

"No," thought Felis, "Stop. Get a grip on yourself. Don't do anything. Think."

Just then the man came walking toward him and stroked his back. It was the wrong moment.

"Not now," said Felis.

Instead of lifting his head, holding out his neck, dropping onto his side, stretching, and all the things Felis normally did out of friendship, he merely turned his head away. A brief purr, out of sheer politeness, that ended almost as soon as it began. Nothing more.

"Can't you see that I'm thinking?" Felis complained. "You act like you own me. You never seem to consider that it might be the other way around."

But the man wouldn't be put off. He wanted to pet Felis, and he wanted Felis to enjoy it. But Felis would not change his mind. He looked at the man briefly and raised a paw. Had the man been a stranger, Felis wouldn't have bothered with a warning, but among friends, this was necessary. "We know each other well enough," thought Felis. Then he swung with his paw.

The man understood immediately. He put on his coat and left. The woman already had her keys in hand. Now Felis had to decide instantly what to do. It was an easy choice. Felis went outside.

The weather was perfect. Not too warm and not

too cold. The sun shone through a hole in the clouds, just the way you want it to when you're planning to take a long trip. On his way to the house next door, Felis checked his yard to see whether everything was in order. Felis loved order and hated it when things changed. Then he searched the neighbor's yard without detecting a trace of Venezia. He sat down and wondered, "She wouldn't have left without me, would she?"

He called for her a few times, but there was no answer. Then he returned home and decided to crawl through the hole in the fence. He had just heard soft footsteps on the other side. But it turned out not to be Venezia. Two tomcats were coming from opposite directions; each stopped short when he noticed the other.

"They're not going to fight, are they? How boring," Felis thought.

Not this time. Somewhat at a loss, the two tomcats sat down and gazed across the green lawn. They waited, the way cats tend to do in these situations.

Suddenly they both rose to leave—but then each sat down again because he had seen the other stand up.

Felis got bored. He settled down beneath the bushes, thinking, "Eventually they've got to give up and go back where they came from."

Minutes passed. Finally the spotted one jumped to his feet and ran away. The white one seemed to have more time. He sat there a while longer, then ambled off.

And so Felis set out again.

On the lawn by the hill, he spotted the white tom for a second time. Relaxed and keeping a proper distance, the tiger cat also waited for prey. Neither seemed to mind when Felis chose a hole and crouched down.

Felis took his time. He could spend an entire day lying in wait beside a mouse hole. When it came to sheer patience he had few equals, especially among the older toms. The white tom quickly left if no victim appeared. The she-cats changed their locations constantly—they always seemed in a hurry to catch something. And Felis had to admit that they were often the most successful. It usually took only a few minutes before a she-cat would trot away, her catch dangling from her mouth. And Felis would still be crouching at an empty hole.

Today Felis succeeded in catching two mice. Actually he should have caught six. But that's the way it goes; with the other toms there, he simply had bad luck.

"Oh, well," said Felis. A good hunter might miss twice but succeeds on the third try. Anyway, too much success makes you impatient the next time. An impatient hunter is a bad hunter.

Felis looked around. The cat with the brown ears sat in the distance, staring in one particular direction.

Felis followed her gaze and saw Venezia. So she hadn't left after all.

Felis felt relieved. But then he remembered the other cats and thought, "I hope all goes well."

And, amazingly, no one even budged. Instead of attacking, the brown-eared cat simply turned her attention back to the mouse hole.

Venezia looked pleased. She greeted Felis.

"I'm glad you're still here," he replied.

Venezia purred.

"Did you notice the sun?" Felis asked. "Just right."

"Yes, just right."

"Then I guess we can leave."

"Leave? But I just got here."

"Not leave. Run away."

"Run away? I see."

"So we can go?"

"In this weather?"

"The weather is just right. You said so yourself."

"Of course it's just right," said Venezia. "So why should we run away?"

"You wanted to run away, didn't you? You started this whole thing."

"Me?"

"Yes, you."

"Not today. Today *you* want to run away."

"Me?" laughed Felis. "If anybody here wants to run away, it's you."

Venezia let her eyes wander and purred. "I still have to think it over," she announced. "It's not so bad here after all. And anyway, tomorrow's Wednesday."

Felis began to purr as well. After a pause, he replied, "Yes, that's true. Someone's expecting us for lunch. It would be very rude not to show up." He looked at Venezia slyly, and they both began to laugh.

141